DISCARD

THE LIBRARY OF WEAPONS OF MASS DESTRUCTION™

Homeland Security *and* Weapons *of* Mass Destruction

How Prepared Are We?

MARK BEYER

The Rosen Publishing Group, Inc., New York

Published in 2005 by The Rosen Publishing Group, Inc.
29 East 21st Street, New York, NY 10010

First Edition

Library of Congress Cataloging-in-Publication Data

Beyer, Mark (Mark T.)
Homeland security and weapons of mass destruction: how prepared are we? / by Mark Beyer.—1st ed.
   p. cm. — (Library of weapons of mass destruction)
Includes bibliographical references and index.
ISBN 1-4042-0289-7 (library binding)
1. Civil defense—United States—Juvenile literature. 2. United States—Defenses—Juvenile literature. 3. Weapons of mass destruction—Juvenile literature. 4. Terrorism—United States—Prevention—Juvenile literature.
I. Title. II. Series.
UA927.B49 2005
363.34'97—dc22

                                                                      2004014610

Manufactured in the United States of America

Cover image: A Coast Guard helicopter patrols near the Statue of Liberty in New York on December 30, 2003, after an increased terror alert was issued by the Department of Homeland Security.

[CONTENTS]

INTRODUCTION

T he United States has, by far, the most powerful military in the history of civilization. Its technological sophistication makes its army, navy, air force, and marine units the most deadly on the planet. No similarly equipped nation has tried to test America's military might by attacking the nation. Other countries know their military strength is no match against such a large and sophisticated force.

Yet the attacks by Al Qaeda hijackers on September 11, 2001, proved that the United

Smoke billows from the Twin Towers after they were struck by airplanes on September 11, 2001. The terror strike was the most deadly attack by a foreign force on the American mainland since 1814, during the War of 1812. It immediately made homeland security the most pressing concern on the national agenda.

States was not prepared to defend its borders against terrorists. Terrorists play by rules that are different from those of national military units. The United States was not attacked by a foreign nation. No army landed on its shores. However, the country was indeed attacked.

Terrorists use small groups to attack nations. Terrorists attack and kill to create fear in the people and the government of a nation. Al Qaeda's hijacking of four commercial airliners and crashing three of them into separate buildings in New York City (World Trade Center towers) and

Alexandria, Virginia (the Pentagon), created the fear that the hijackers intended. (The fourth plane was supposedly meant to strike the Capitol in Washington, D.C. It crashed, instead, onto a field in Pennsylvania after hijackers brought down the plane to prevent advancing passengers from gaining control.)

Al Qaeda's 9/11 attacks were not the group's first strike against the United States. Al Qaeda was responsible for the 1993 bombing of the World Trade Center as well. Of course, foreign terrorists were not responsible for the attack on the FBI building in Oklahoma City in 1994. That terrorist attack came from a former U.S. Army private, Timothy McVeigh. He was a white male in his late twenties who had previously been associated with a white supremacist group.

Both of these earlier attacks proved two things. The first is that no amount of military strength could have prevented either attack. The second is that the United States' law enforcement agencies were ill-prepared to stop the attacks before they happened. After September 11, 2001, it quickly became apparent that the federal government needed to do something to better protect U.S. citizens. It also needed to better prepare the various law enforcement and intelligence agencies to deal with possible future attacks against the United States.

On September 21, 2001, President George W. Bush opened the Office of Homeland Security in the White House. He named as its director Pennsylvania governor Tom Ridge. Bush also proposed forming a cabinet-level Department of Homeland Security. It would combine twenty-two separate agencies under one umbrella leadership. The Department of Homeland Security (DHS) would coordinate intelligence, law enforcement, immigration, travel, and border safety (to name a few) at the highest levels to make the country more secure against attacks from abroad or within its borders. It would also make the country more prepared to respond to another deadly attack.

By November 2002, Congress had voted to establish the Department of Homeland Security. Several years have passed since the organization of this newest federal agency. The task of bringing together twenty-two separate agencies is complete. The design to

Supreme Court justice Clarence Thomas *(left)* swears in Tom Ridge *(center)* to head the Office of Homeland Security during a ceremony at the White House on October 8, 2001. Looking on are President Bush *(second from left)* and Ridge's wife, Michele; son, Tom; and daughter, Lesley. A Vietnam veteran, Ridge worked as a private lawyer and later as an assistant district attorney before entering politics. He served seven terms in Congress before becoming governor of Pennsylvania in 1995.

share information within the department has finally been put into place. Money has been approved for the agency and sent to hundreds of subagencies at the federal, state, and local levels. Yet one question lingers among many citizens and experts alike: are we any safer or more prepared than we were before September 11, 2001?

The federal government, most state governments, and many local agencies claim that the country is safer and better prepared to defend against or respond to another terrorist attack. Many private organizations agree. However, many experts and other private organizations—and a lot of public agencies and some local and state governments—claim we are not any safer today than we were on September 10, 2001.

So who is right? Are all the pieces now in place to defend against another major terrorist attack? In the event of such an attack, are response units better prepared to deal with coordinated bombings, the use of biological or chemical weapons against cities, or even a nuclear device set off in a major metropolitan area? The evidence seems to suggest a yes-and-no answer. It depends on whom you talk to and what part of the safety question is under discussion. This book looks at both sides of the argument and at homeland safety in general. If the facts of a yes-or-no answer are any indication of truth behind the question, "Are we safe?" then one needs to look at three basic parts of the system: intelligence, law enforcement, and funding. Has intelligence improved? Has law enforcement improved? Is there enough money to ensure that every part of the homeland security structure works when it is supposed to? ■

On October 1, 2003, President George W. Bush signed into law the Homeland Security Appropriations Act at the Department of Homeland Security. The act committed $31 billion to the new department. During the ceremony, President Bush said, "Oceans no longer protect us from danger. And we're taking unprecedented measures to prevent terrorist attacks, reduce our vulnerability and to prepare for any emergency."

PROTECTING THE HOMELAND

THE DEPARTMENT OF HOMELAND SECURITY

The U.S. Congress passed the Homeland Security Act in November 2002. This law upgraded the Office of Homeland Security to a cabinet-level department. As the head of a cabinet-level department, the secretary of homeland security reports directly to the president. All agencies within the new department report directly to the secretary.

This chain of command prevents the usual long hierarchy of supervisors that often holds up important information and decisions. With terrorism and its potential to create of-the-moment problems, quick decisions are essential to get people to act quickly. Equally important, by combining twenty-two federal agencies to be directed by a single cabinet secretary, the federal government hopes to move intelligence to the proper agencies, direct people and resources without multiple levels of command, and respond to threats and attacks more quickly.

This structure was important to the new department because of the three major terrorist attacks that had happened on U.S. soil during the previous nine years. Lapses in intelligence, law enforcement, immigration, and travel safety each created the opportunity for the success of the Oklahoma City bombing, the first World Trade Center bombing in 1993, and the September 11 attacks. President Bush and Congress decided that a coordinated effort among close to two dozen federal agencies, hundreds of state agencies, and thousands of local municipalities across the nation was crucial for future success against further attacks.

MISSION STATEMENT AND STRATEGIES

The National Homeland Security Strategy was published in July 2002, four months before Congress enacted the Homeland Security Act. All parts of government and the nation could review how the proposed department was to be structured, what were to be its main objectives, and what were included in each new subagency's responsibilities. According to the Department of Homeland Security's Web site, its primary missions include:

> Preventing terrorist attacks within the United States, reducing the vulnerability of the United States to terrorism at home, and minimizing the damage and assisting in the recovery from any attacks that may occur. The Department's primary responsibilities correspond to the five major functions established by the bill within the

> Department: information analysis and infrastructure protection; chemical, biological, radiological, nuclear, and related countermeasures; border and transportation security; emergency preparedness and response; and coordination with other parts of the federal government, with state and local governments, and with the private sector.

To do this, the department consolidated twenty-two existing federal agencies. These agencies employ more than 180,000 federal workers. In some capacity, each agency consolidated under the act has security-related jobs. These include duties such as agricultural research, port safety and defense, and immigration monitoring and control. Guiding all these efforts today is the secretary of homeland security, Tom Ridge.

One of the department's strategies is to divide the duties of these various agencies into five subagencies, called directorates. They are Border and Transportation Security, Emergency Preparedness and Response, Science and Technology, Information Analysis and Infrastructure Protection, and Management. Two agencies, the Coast Guard and the Secret Service, were transferred into the department from the Transportation and Treasury Departments, respectively. The department also brings under its umbrella of control the Transportation Security Administration, agencies of the Customs Service, the Immigration and Naturalization Service, and even parts of the Federal Bureau of Investigation (FBI). The department will not include the vast majority of the FBI or any part of the Central Intelligence Agency (CIA). Each of these departments has specifically outlined duties.

Of course, none of these directorates within the Department of Homeland Security is new. Their tasks have not changed dramatically from what they had been all along. The difference is that their efforts are coordinated within the broader agency so that information is shared in order to better protect against terrorist threats and respond to attacks.

A customs and border protection agent checks a foreign visitor's image and fingerprints against a terrorist watch list on a computer database at New York City's JFK airport. The database is part of a system called US-VISIT (United States Visitor and Immigrant Status Indicator Technology), which is being implemented at 115 American airports and 14 seaports.

BORDER AND TRANSPORTATION SECURITY

The Border and Transportation Security (BTS) directorate has a budget of $18 billion and employs approximately 156,200 agents. The BTS has the tasks of managing and protecting the borders and transportation systems within the United States. These include those within U.S. territories overseas.

The Department of Homeland Security's Web site defines the BTS's duties as:

> (1) preventing the entry of terrorists and the instruments of terrorism into the United States, (2) securing the borders, territorial waters, ports, terminals, waterways, and air, land, and sea transportation systems of the United States, (3) administering the immigration and naturalization laws of the United States, including the establishment of rules governing the granting of visas and other forms of permission to enter the

United States to individuals who are not citizens or lawful permanent residents, (4) administering the customs laws of the United States, and (5) ensuring the speedy, orderly, and efficient flow of lawful traffic and commerce in carrying out these responsibilities.

EMERGENCY PREPAREDNESS AND RESPONSE

The Emergency Preparedness and Response (EPR) directorate has a budget of $6 billion and employs nearly 5,300 agents. The directorate combines the former Federal Emergency Management Agency, the FBI's National Domestic Preparedness Office, and the Energy Department's Nuclear Incident Response team. The EPR's duties include:

(1) helping to ensure the preparedness of emergency response providers for terrorist attacks, major disasters, and other emergencies, (2) establishing standards, conducting exercises and training, evaluating performance, and providing funds in relation to the Nuclear Incident Response, (3) providing the federal government's response to terrorist attacks and major disasters, (4) aiding the recovery from terrorist attacks and major disasters, (5) working with other federal and non-federal agencies to build a comprehensive national incident management system, (6) consolidating existing federal government emergency response plans into a single, coordinated national response plan, and (7) developing comprehensive programs for developing interoperative communications technology and ensuring that emergency response providers acquire such technology.

SCIENCE AND TECHNOLOGY

The Science and Technology directorate is also known as the Directorate for Chemical, Biological, Radiological, and Nuclear Countermeasures. It leads the national job of preparing for and responding to terrorist threats using chemical, biological, radiological, and nuclear weapons. These weapons are considered weapons of mass

The Plum Island Animal Disease Center was transferred into the Department of Homeland Security in June 2003 because the U.S. government recognized the threat of terrorists using animal diseases to kill Americans and disrupt the American economy. Located on New York's Plum Island, the center is the only place in the United States where highly infectious foreign diseases are studied. Although it boasts a safety record of not allowing a single pathogen to escape from the island in its fifty-plus-year history, the center faces allegations that it was the source of the Lyme disease and the West Nile virus outbreaks in the United States.

destruction (WMD) because of their potential to kill thousands of people in a single attack.

This directorate is also responsible for developing diagnostics, vaccines, antibodies, antidotes, and other remedies to protect or counter the effects of a WMD attack. Scientific research plays a significant role within the Science and Technology directorate. It brings together the federal government's research organizations. These include the Lawrence Livermore National Laboratory and the Plum Island Animal Disease Center. Lawrence Livermore Laboratory researches nuclear, chemical, and biological substances and their effects on people (along with potential prevention and antidotes). The Plum Island labs work to protect the U.S. food market from foreign animal diseases, including foot-and-mouth disease and mad cow disease.

The Science and Technology directorate employs nearly 600 agents and has a budget of $803 million.

INFORMATION ANALYSIS AND INFRASTRUCTURE PROTECTION

The budget to fund the Information Analysis and Infrastructure Protection directorate is $829 million. It employs nearly 976 agents who are split between two main units: Threat Analysis and Warning, and Critical Infrastructure Protection.

Threat Analysis and Warning collects all information from the many different U.S. intelligence agencies (and foreign agencies sharing information) to identify and judge whether the threat is real. It also evaluates whether the threat should be acted upon and what level of action should be taken. These participating and information-sharing agencies include the FBI, CIA, National Security Agency (NSA), Defense Intelligence Agency, and the Drug Enforcement Agency (DEA).

Included in its analysis is judgment of the United States' vulnerability against particular threats. Once a threat has been identified, the department assesses the

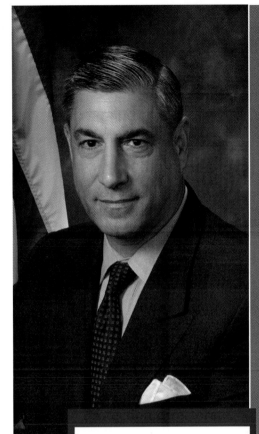

Frank Libutti is the Department of Homeland Security's undersecretary for the Information Analysis and Infrastructure Protection directorate. Prior to his appointment in 2003, he was the New York City Police Department's deputy commander of counter-terrorism.

Pictured on March 6, 2002, this buoy security system was installed at the Lake of the Ozarks, Missouri, near Bagnell Dam, to guard against potential terrorist attacks. The underwater security system helps protect the dam's eight fifty-ton concrete turbines, which supply electricity to many consumers in Missouri and Illinois.

target's vulnerability. This allows the department to then issue a warning and recommend action to protect the structures under threat and people who may be within or near the area.

Critical Infrastructure Protection provides security information estimates about what the department terms "internal systems." These systems relate to almost every facet of normal life in the United States, such as food markets, water supply and systems, emergency services, health and sanitation systems, energy systems, information and tele-communications networks, banking and finance institutions, and transportation systems.

In addition, the Information Analysis and Infrastructure Protection directorate must also guard U.S. energy, transportation, chemical, and defense industries. The postal and shipping systems fall under the directorate's protection, as do all national monuments.

MANAGEMENT

Of course, any agency this large must be managed itself. With so many employees, computer systems, information networks, and hundreds (if not thousands) of field offices, there would be chaos without proper procedures. The Management directorate oversees getting money from Congress and making it available to every subagency in the Department of Homeland Security. It also purchases equipment and hires agents and other personnel. It is responsible for information and technology systems used throughout the department. It also plans and implements security procedures to protect personnel, properties, equipment, technology systems, and other resources. Finally, the Management directorate identifies and tracks the perform-ances of each subagency and those offices within it.

ANALYZING THE DEPARTMENT

Critics quickly pointed out the flaws of such a large agency with so many specific and different functions. They list its size, scope of responsibilities, and budget among their concerns. These critics included members of Congress, state governors, major city mayors, and local officials such as police and fire chiefs. These people have an informed view of the department's weaknesses because they will be the ones who get the money to the department; distribute the money to the states, cities, and local agencies in need; hire and train people; purchase materials and equipment; or do the actual work of investigating problems, preparing for attacks, and responding to attacks when and where they occur.

In the following chapters, we shall learn about individual threats to the nation, how the department will respond to them, and read expert judgments on the structure and functioning of the department. Critical to understanding the department's potential for success is being aware of just how much money is needed to secure the homeland, who gets this money, and how the money is distributed. █

2

CHEMICAL AND BIOLOGICAL WEAPONS

Chemical weapons are laboratory-made solutions of chemicals that cause great harm to the human body, and even death. Mustard gas and sarin are perhaps the most widely known chemical weapons. Both are spread through aerosol means. They are sprayed in a certain area to affect people there. Most chemical weapons react within a person's respiratory system. When a victim inhales the chemical sprayed in a fine mist, the poison affects the central nervous system. These weapons stop a person's breathing or cause limbs to stop functioning as a result of interference in brain activity. Without proper antidotes given within a certain amount of time, victims will die. Those who survive are often left blind or mentally impaired, or they suffer from long-term illnesses such as a constant cough, joint pain, or major organ malfunction.

Biological weapons include anthrax, bubonic plague, ricin, and even polio. They are different from chemical agents in that they are organic, meaning they occur naturally in the environment. Generally, biological weapons affect the human body differently than the fast-acting chemical agents. Most biological agents have an incubation period, during which the germ or virus has time to take hold in the body. When the person becomes infected, he or she can often pass the germ or virus on to other people. For this reason, biological weapons are generally considered more dangerous than chemical weapons.

Dozens of nations have chemical and biological weapons (CBWs). Dozens more terrorist groups may be trying to buy them from some of these countries. Terrorist groups might even be trying to make CBWs themselves. Although CBWs are difficult to make and release against a large number of people, they are considered effective terrorist weapons because of the fear that they can strike in a population. Knowing who has them, how they are used, and how they might be brought into the United States is another job of the Department of Homeland Security.

WHO HAS CHEMICAL AND BIOLOGICAL WEAPONS?

The U.S. government lists twenty-eight countries it believes have or have had chemical and/or biological weapons. Countries included on this list are North Korea, Iraq, Algeria, Cuba, Ethiopia, and Egypt. The U.S. intelligence agencies admit that they know for certain of CBW stockpiles or

U.S. Capitol police, dressed in protective gear, remove mail from the Hart Senate Office Building on February 5, 2004, after it was revealed that a letter containing ricin addressed to the White House was intercepted by federal officials.

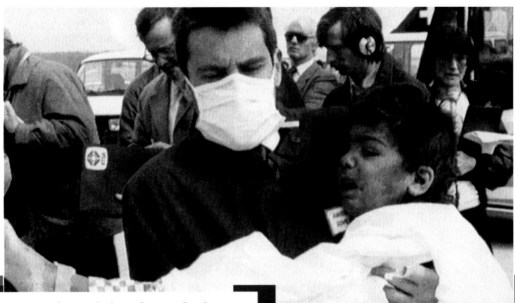

An injured Kurdish girl is rushed to a waiting ambulance upon her arrival in Geneva, Switzerland. She was one of many victims of a nerve gas attack on the predominantly Kurdish population in Halabja, Iraq, in 1988. Shortly after Iraqi warplanes dropped several bombs on the village, the villagers began to experience breathing difficulties, watery eyes, vomiting, and skin blisters.

programs in fewer than half those countries. That means that there could be tons of chemical and biological weapons hidden somewhere within those twenty-eight countries. Some of that amount may be available on the black market to the highest bidder.

HOW CHEMICAL AND BIOLOGICAL WEAPONS ARE USED

The good news is that the most deadly chemical and biological weapons are difficult to make. They are even harder to distribute to a large population. Part of the problem for countries—and terrorist organizations especially—involved in weapons programs of this sort is the advanced technology needed to produce effective weapons of mass destruction.

MANUFACTURE AND USE OF CHEMICAL WEAPONS

Countries and terrorists can use simple base chemicals, such as chlorine and hydrogen cyanide, as weapons. For nerve agents, however, a

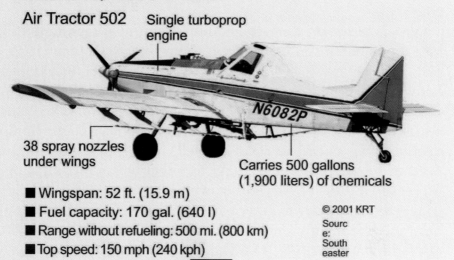

Crop-dusting airplane

Some of the terrorists who hijacked airliners Sept. 11 tried to gain access to crop dusters in Florida.

Air Tractor 502

Single turboprop engine

N6082P

38 spray nozzles under wings

Carries 500 gallons (1,900 liters) of chemicals

- Wingspan: 52 ft. (15.9 m)
- Fuel capacity: 170 gal. (640 l)
- Range without refueling: 500 mi. (800 km)
- Top speed: 150 mph (240 kph)

© 2001 KRT

Source: Southeaster

weapons-quality program requires a high level of expertise in the study and manufacture of chemicals. One cannot simply buy lab equipment and start mixing chemicals in a basement. Such operations would produce nothing of quality to kill humans either on a battlefield or distributed in a populated area. The most probable effect of basement technology would be the killing of the scientists themselves.

This illustration provides technical information about a typical crop-dusting airplane, including its capacity to carry and spread chemicals. Allegations that the 9/11 terrorists tried to get loans to finance crop-dusting companies led to several emergency bans on crop dusting in the months following the 9/11 attacks.

High-grade nerve agents require special corrosive-resistant containers for manufacture. These include reactors, degassers, distillation columns, and additional equipment made of high nickel alloys or other metals. All are needed to contain the corrosive chemicals and by-products of their production. The trouble for countries or terrorists wanting this equipment is that it is not sold to just anyone or any country.

Even if terrorists were to acquire chemical weapons, getting them into the country and distributing them to a large population is difficult. The two most common ways to distribute chemical weapons are bombs or aerosol sprays. Aerosol spraying of chemical weapons requires airplanes to cover large areas. However, once the chemical is released into the air, the wind takes it along its own route. Bombs could distribute the chemical agent as well. However, many bombs would need to be set off around a city to affect a large number of people. Moreover, if these bombs are set off in the open air, the people most in danger are those downwind of the explosion. Chemical weapons have been used frequently since their first, large-scale use on the battlefields of World War I (1914–1918). The most recent cases have been Saddam Hussein's gassing of the Kurds in the Iraqi village of Halabja in 1988, and the Japanese cult Aum Shinrikyo releasing sarin nerve gas inside a Tokyo subway in 1995.

MANUFACTURE AND USE OF BIOLOGICAL WEAPONS

Biological weapons are very different in scope from chemical weapons when it comes to manufacture and use. Where low-grade chemical weapons can still harm or even kill people, poorly manufactured biological weapons are useless. The main reason for this is that biological weapons are living organisms: viruses and spores that need to be alive when they enter a victim's body. Manufacturing weapons-quality biological weapons requires that same high level of expertise required to produce chemical weapons. In addition, lab equipment and manufacturing machinery are difficult to purchase because these items are on protective lists that outline who can and cannot purchase them.

Distributing biological weapons can be even more difficult than chemical weapons. If released in the atmosphere, biological agents have a high likelihood of dying as soon as they hit the air. This is because ultraviolet light kills these organisms. Also, biological weapons released in the air are subject to control by winds. The

4TH GRADE
GREENDALE SCHOOL
FRANKLIN PARK NJ 08852

SENATOR DASCHLE
509 HART SENATE OFFICE
BUILDING
WASHINGTON D.C. 2053

Five people died as a result of exposure to anthrax that was sent through the U.S. mail in September and October 2001. The Federal Bureau of Investigation (FBI) believes an American, rather than foreign terrorists, was behind the anthrax attacks.

most effective way to distribute biological weapons is in a small, controlled environment. For example, the envelopes containing anthrax sent to Senator Patrick Leahy, NBC newscaster Tom Brokaw, and the *New York Times* building in the weeks following the 9/11 attacks each kept the packaged spores within an enclosed building. By doing this, the terrorist was assured that the envelopes would be at least opened, and possibly then handled, by several people before the substance was discovered. This allowed the anthrax spores to be picked up by air currents and then distributed throughout the building by the ventilation system. Several people died from this terrorist attack, but not the hundreds or thousands as a country or terrorist organization might have wanted.

HOW THE DEPARTMENT OF HOMELAND SECURITY DEALS WITH CBWS

The Department of Homeland Security is devising plans to develop and distribute vaccines, antidotes, and emergency services in the event

GET A KIT

Water & Food | Clean Air | First Aid Kit | Portable Kit
Supply Checklists | Special Needs Items

When preparing for a possible emergency situation, it's best to think first about the basics of survival: **fresh water, food, clean air and warmth**.

WATER & FOOD
Find out how to store and prepare for at least three days of survival.

PORTABLE KIT
Supplies items essential for survival.

CLEAN AIR
Learn how to improvise with what you have on hand to protect your mouth, nose, eyes and cuts in your skin.

SUPPLY CHECKLISTS
Assemble clothing & bedding, tools and other basic supplies.

SPECIAL NEEDS ITEMS
Lists for those with special needs—babies, adults, seniors and people with disabilities.

FIRST AID KIT
Knowing how to treat minor injuries can make a difference in an emergency. If you have these basic supplies you are better prepared to help your loved ones when they are hurt.

This Web page from the Department of Homeland Security's Web site offers tips to the general public on preparing for an emergency. The department bears the responsibility of educating the public, on a continuing basis, about how to be prepared in case of a national emergency. Using the slogan "Don't Be Afraid, Be Ready," the department's Web site (http://www.ready.gov) also encourages citizens to be active participants in helping prevent terror attacks.

of a CBW attack. The department uses agencies and programs from the Department of Health and Human Services, as well as certain relevant programs and activities of the Department of Energy, the National Bio-Weapons Defense Analysis Center, and the Plum Island Animal Disease Center.

Investigating agents from the CIA, FBI, NSA, and border patrol look into terrorist cells' ability to purchase and/or bring CBW materials into the United States. Analysis of data discovered about all terrorist cells as they relate to CBWs is critical. Also important is the sharing of information should an attack plan be discovered.

Apart from its investigation and interdiction duties, the department is putting a lot of energy into preparedness activities. One level of preparation involves first responders, who are the police, fire, and emergency medical units first on the scene of any related CBW attack. These agencies have plans in place to prepare people, buildings, and emergency units in case of a threat or following an attack. Each has been practicing preparedness for such events for years. Today, however, the preparation is more urgent because of 9/11.

> "Take the time, be informed, then go about the business of enjoying your family and enjoying America."
>
> *Tom Ridge*

The other preparation designs include the general public. On February 19, 2003, Secretary Tom Ridge spoke to PBS newscaster Jim Lehrer about a new kind of ready plan in which all Americans should participate. Ridge said, "There are three basic recommendations that we make[:] have a communication plan with your family . . . an emergency supply kit . . . and the third is just a real message for the adults: Take the time, be informed, then go about the business of enjoying your family and enjoying America." The crux of the message was for families to be aware of where each member might be in case of a terrorist attack. This is to ensure that families are able to plan to reunite after an attack.

WHAT THE CRITICS SAY

Several expert critics have given their opinion on the way the Department of Homeland Security has gone about preparing the nation for possible terrorist attacks. Zbigniew Brzezinski, former adviser to the John Kennedy, Lyndon Johnson, and Jimmy Carter administrations on military and foreign policy, made the following comments about a preparedness exercise during a *NewsHour with Jim Lehrer* interview on March 20, 2003:

> [Citizens are] overprepared in the sense that I think [the government is] creating an atmosphere of panic in the country, which is unhealthy. We can't anticipate all terrorist acts. They may occur from time to time; in a number of countries in recent years, there have been a lot of terrorist activity, but they have learned to live with it and to cope with it. We have been struck once, very badly. But since then, I think we have been hyping the issue, both in the mass media and the government. And I think it is creating a situation which is quite unhealthy . . . I think the government has been pumping up the terrorist business to an excessive degree. If we are really serious about it, we would greatly increase our intelligence capabilities because that's the best protection—but not orange codes or other colored codes, periodic announcements, huge massive bureaucracy, tens of billions of dollars. We can't protect everything anyway but we can induce so much fear in our society that something very precious is going to be lost.

> "I think [the government is] creating an atmosphere of panic in the country, which is unhealthy."
>
> *Zbigniew Brzezinski*

Other critics include average citizens who partook in a mock terrorist attack using biological weapons (plague) in Maywood, Illinois, in May 2003. Mock patients suffering from effects of the plague entered Loyola University Medical Center. Max Margolis, a mock patient had this to say about his treatment: "They [the emergency medical staff] took us all at once and didn't ask what symptoms we had or any problems that were going on. So they just took us all together, so people were dying

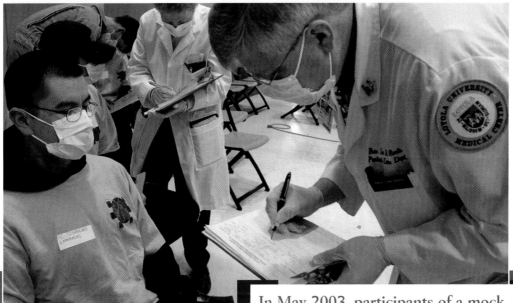

In May 2003, participants of a mock bioterrorism disaster performed a screening for symptoms at Loyola University Medical Center in Maywood, Illinois. Mock drills such as this one are useful in identifying weaknesses in emergency response policies and procedures.

over here. People were dying over there, and they didn't even know what the problems were." Chicago's WTTW newscaster Elizabeth Brackett gave her assessment of the homeland security readiness plan: "Had it been real, it would have been a devastating week for the United States."

In a concluding remark to the exercise, political scientist Matthew Lippman said during the same WTTW news report: "At the same time that we're spending roughly $16 million on this exercise, and where the public health system is central, we're not funding the public health system." This assessment has been echoed across the country, in places where the mock drills have been held.

Obviously, the plans now in place for America's preparedness against terrorist attacks need refining and additional practice. This is something the department is further instituting each week. ■

3

NUCLEAR AND RADIOLOGICAL WEAPONS

Since 1997, speculation over the possibility of missing atomic bombs the size of a suitcase in the former Soviet Union has caused a great deal of concern among international policing agencies. More than 100 one-kiloton atomic bombs are said to be missing from the stockpile once maintained by the former Soviet Union.

This handheld instrument, called a RadNet, combines a cellular phone, radiation sensors, personal digital assistant, and global positioning system to allow homeland security agents to detect radiation and communicate the data quickly.

In addition, radiological material is used in hundreds of different manufacturing systems, military hardware, and medical facilities. If even a few ounces of this material were to be used in a so-called dirty bomb, the effects to people, property, and even the future of a city would be catastrophic.

The Department of Homeland Security investigates such devices. It tries to identify who might have them or might be trying to buy or make them. It also tries to prepare the United States' first responders and the general public in case of attack. Yet, to fully appreciate the dangers of these weapons, knowing what they are, who has them, and how they can be used is important to understanding the department's awesome task.

HOW NUCLEAR AND RADIOLOGICAL WEAPONS ARE USED

Nuclear bombs work by creating a chain reaction within highly radioactive material. When this chain reaction is triggered, a huge

Russian employees work to make a fleet of nuclear submarines harmless at a U.S.-funded nuclear waste facility in Severodvinsk, Russia. Founded one year before the September 11 attacks, the facility has gained new importance as the United States increases its efforts to minimize the chance of terrorists getting their hands on nuclear materials from former Soviet states.

The Al-Tuwaitha nuclear facility outside Baghdad, Iraq, was looted after the fall of Saddam Hussein's government in 2003. Barrels of radioactive material were stolen from the plant, some of which were never recovered. Above is a portrait of Mohamed el-Baradei, head of the International Atomic Energy Agency, which tracks the illegal development of nuclear weapons around the world.

amount of energy is released in an explosion. The blast itself is powerful enough to kill people and destroy structures with its force and heat. The radioactive material released into the atmosphere kills people through radiation sickness immediately (with high doses) or later in life through cancer (with lower doses). The worst part about nuclear weapons is that radiation is left behind, which makes the land, buildings, and environment uninhabitable for hundreds or even thousands of years.

Radiological weapons are not as powerful as nuclear bombs. They are used more to "dirty" an environment to make it unusable to people. Its blast will kill far fewer people. The radiation dispersed upon detonation could also harm humans through radiation sickness immediately (depending on dosage level at the blast) or, again, later in life. The U.S. government is most concerned about the dirty bomb—also known as a radiological dispersal device (RDD)—which would be a potent instrument of terror to Americans. For example, imagine a suicide bomber with dynamite strapped to his chest, but wrapped inside that dynamite is a pound of radioactive material. An attack like this could leave an area as large as a square mile unusable for centuries.

WHO HAS NUCLEAR AND RADIOLOGICAL WEAPONS?

There are now nine countries that have nuclear weapons: Britain, China, France, India, Israel, North Korea, Pakistan, Russia, and the United States. Also, the world knows of the possibility of missing suitcase-size nuclear bombs. Intelligence communities around the world, in compliance with international treaties aimed at preventing the spread of nuclear weapons, monitor the number and testing of these deadly bombs. Of course, often the technology to design nuclear power facilities, and even nuclear research laboratories, is sold to nonmember nations. However, the use of one or more of the thousands of bombs in the world is unlikely as an action of war. The reasons for this include the likelihood that whatever nation next uses a nuclear bomb will itself be bombed.

Radiological weapons are a different story altogether. Because conventional explosives can be used with radioactive material (albeit not containing such dangerous levels of radiation as found in nuclear bombs), the possibility of a dirty bomb being used is increasing daily. Intelligence agencies such as the CIA, NSA, and the International Atomic Energy Agency (IAEA) know that these materials exist in various nations in the Middle East and Africa, including Somalia, Sudan, Ethiopia, and Uganda.

HOW THE DHS INVESTIGATES NUCLEAR TERROR

The Science and Technology directorate conducts intelligence investigations into the possible theft and/or sale of nuclear material by public, private, or government agents to terrorists. The directorate uses intelligence from the FBI, CIA, NSA, and IAEA. Information sharing will be critical if terrorists are to be stopped from importing nuclear material into the country (or stealing it from U.S. sources).

One complication to this job is the amount of radiological material already used for perfectly legal means, such as medical equipment, in many countries. Intelligence agencies worldwide know that people have stolen some of this material. One recent episode involved the U.S. war in Iraq. During the fall of Baghdad, nuclear facilities were not

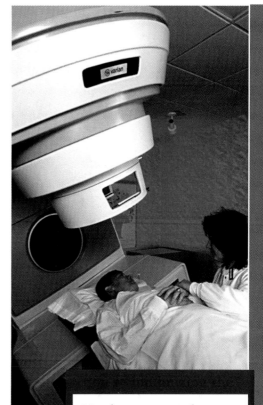

Nuclear materials are increasingly being used in diagnosing and treating life-threatening illnesses such as cancer. In addition to minimizing the risk of overexposure to both patient and medical personnel, hospitals must follow strict guidelines in monitoring and disposing of these materials to avoid them falling into the wrong hands.

secured by the military. When mass looting occurred during and
after the battle for the city, radioactive material went missing in the
hands of looters. What has happened to that material? Might some
of it already have been sold to terrorists? These are questions the
Department of Homeland Security—and international police and
intelligence agencies—are concerned about. ■

Thousands of passenger vehicles wait to cross the Mexican border
into the United States at the Bridge of the Americas port of entry in
El Paso, Texas, on October 19, 2001. Since the September 11 attacks,
border inspections have become more rigid, increasing the average
waiting time for drivers to between forty-five minutes and three
hours, depending on the time of day.

ASSESSING THE PREPAREDNESS OF HOMELAND SECURITY

The Bush administration says that the Department of Homeland Security will work smoothly and efficiently given time. Secretary Tom Ridge told reporters at his swearing-in news conference that the department would take a year to completely coordinate all the directorates and subagencies under its umbrella management. In February 2004, Ridge told the host of PBS's *The NewsHour with Jim Lehrer* that in another year the department would have put into place the proper system where all intelligence gathered by U.S. agencies will be available to every department in need of such information.

Experts outside of the government say this is a tall order. For one thing, the FBI and CIA have never shared information properly or smoothly. There seems to be a wall between the two agencies. One reason for this wall is that the CIA, by law, cannot spy on Americans inside the country or conduct investigations within the United States. That is the job of the FBI.

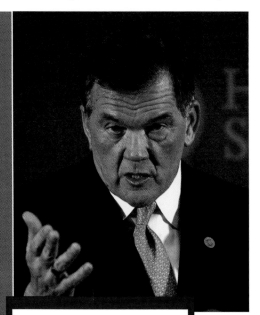

Tom Ridge testifies before the Senate Appropriations Committee about the Department of Homeland Security's 2005 budget on February 10, 2004. The size of the department's budget and how it is allocated attracts much of the criticism of the government's approach to homeland security.

Other experts claim the whole structure of homeland security is dependent on money and politics. Private organizations whose sole job is to analyze the government have computed the numbers on who gets what money and how the money gets to those in most need. Their assessment shows a system of government agencies sorely lacking in money and equipment with which to properly do their jobs.

Secretary Tom Ridge has claimed that the Department of Homeland Security is operating as an agency of its type should. He describes it as being fully staffed and funded, properly trained, with the best intelligence possible, and prepared to protect, defend, and respond to terrorist attacks. Of course, this is what government is supposed to do. If these

SECURING THE BORDERS AND TRANSPORTATION SAFETY

The immediate reaction of the federal government to the 9/11 attacks was to secure all borders and increase security at all airports. Secretary Ridge accepted the order by President Bush to make a plan to reopen airports and ensure airline safety as soon as possible. This plan was put into effect as soon as airports reopened within seven days following the attacks. This response intensified as the months went by.

Congress took a further step by passing the Aviation and Transportation Security Act in October 2001, which outlined measures to increase security, hire more screening personnel, and purchase bomb-scanning machines for every major airport in the country. Billions of dollars have gone into securing airports to assure passengers of airline safety. Today, all screening personnel are federal employees who have gone through a rigorous hiring process. Since January 1, 2003, every piece of luggage checked onto a flight is checked for explosives using mechanical detection devices, bomb-sniffing dogs, or physical searches.

Dramatic changes have also taken place at America's borders. Checks of every passport against its carrier are now done (something that was lax in the days before 9/11). Physical inspections of the millions of vehicles that cross the borders each day have also increased. A computer system to check all passports against lists of possible terrorists is in the works, but it will take time to get it up and running. The federal government had not seen this as a priority. However, it must now play catch-up to bring all information online. It will take time, however, before America's border can truly be considered safe. The hardware systems, computer programs, personnel training, and, of course, all that data entry must be implemented to ensure every safety precaution is in place.

An airport security agent searches a traveler as his shoes roll off the conveyor belt of an X-ray machine at the Eastern Iowa Airport in Cedar Rapids on December 24, 2001. Shoe inspections have become routine since a suspected terrorist was arrested for having a bomb implanted into his shoes, which authorities believe he had planned to detonate during a flight.

tasks are all done properly, even when a terrorist strike occurs, the country will be prepared. Assessing how the department actually works in such a situation is one way of determining its overall preparedness.

INFORMATION GATHERING

A five-level, color-coded threat assessment system was put into place in March 2002. Since then, numerous warnings of different levels have been given. Some have been made nationwide, such as the one on September 10, 2002, just a day short of the first anniversary of the 9/11 attacks. Other warning elevations have been given to specific cities, such as the one that took place in August 2002, when security was raised around San Francisco's Golden Gate Bridge after a specific threat was confirmed.

The threats that force the elevation of the color-coded system come from many sources. Mostly, however, they come from intercepted communications between terrorist cells. These interceptions are called "chatter." The National Security Agency commands several dozen listening posts around the world. James Bamford, author of *Body of Secrets: Anatomy of the Ultra-Secret National Security Agency*, spoke about information gathering and translation during a PBS *NewsHour* interview on November 14, 2002. He said:

> An average listening post . . . picks up about two million pieces of communication an hour. That's telephone calls, the e-mail, faxes, data transmissions, and then they use filters to try to pull out just what the information is that they want. They want information that's to and from these cells or to and from certain people in Kandahar or in Afghanistan or Kabul or in Yemen.

This information gathering is time-consuming, and so threats are difficult to assess immediately.

Bamford also noted: "Before September 11, [2001,] there were several times when the volume increased tremendously. They weren't able to pin down exactly when or where the terrorist incident was going to take place, but they were aware that there was probably something that was going to be happening in the near future."

Part of the problem with threat assessment is translating the intercepted communications. As Bamford explained, the NSA has found it difficult hiring adequate linguists in recent years. The effect of this translation problem was apparent after the 9/11 attacks. Just a day before the attacks, critical information came from suspected terrorists but was not translated until after the attacks.

The Bush administration and Secretary Ridge claim that no specific information has ever really come through to pinpoint the exact date, time, and location of a threat. This is true. However, with enough information gathered during routine investigation and by sharing that information with other agencies, threats can be found out before they become attacks.

Two examples illustrate how communications can succeed or fail, depending on the desire of the individuals on the job and the protocols in place. An FBI agent in Phoenix, Arizona, had information on Zacarias Moussaoui, who has been linked to the 9/11 attacks, in the

HOMELAND SECURITY ADVISORY SYSTEM

SEVERE
SEVERE RISK OF TERRORIST ATTACKS

HIGH
HIGH RISK OF TERRORIST ATTACKS

ELEVATED
SIGNIFICANT RISK OF TERRORIST ATTACKS

GUARDED
GENERAL RISK OF TERRORIST ATTACKS

LOW
LOW RISK OF TERRORIST ATTACKS

This is the five-level, color-coded terrorist alert that the Homeland Security Department has used since March 12, 2002. It was developed in response to public complaints that the broad terror warnings issued by the federal government after September 11, 2001, raised alarms without providing useful information. Many critics contend that the new system does not solve that problem.

Zacarias Moussaoui is often referred to as the twentieth hijacker because it is widely believed that he was supposed to have been on one of the flights used to conduct the September 11 attacks but failed to make it because he had been arrested several weeks earlier.

summer of 2001. She had observed that Moussaoui tried to learn how to fly a jumbo jet by buying time to use a flight simulator. She had sent that information to a superior. That information was never passed on to any other U.S. intelligence or law enforcement agency, and it wasn't even relayed to the FBI director's office. Had Moussaoui been investigated, could the September 11, 2001, attacks been found out? Some experts say probably. But without that sharing of information, U.S. agencies don't even get a chance to stop terrorists from striking.

The second example comes from more than a year after the 9/11 attacks. By then, new guidelines on information gathering and law enforcement had been distributed to agencies nationwide. In New York City, harbor police stopped three people in a fishing boat taking pictures of ferries crossing New York Harbor. A quick investigation took place, but nothing was found to be illegal. Yet afterward, the so-called fishermen's story was taken apart and the police realized that they had not been fishing. When police went to the address given by the fishermen, the apartment was empty. The men were tracked to Pennsylvania. When two of them were caught, they were found to be illegal immigrants. They were deported. The lesson here is that people will not stop their activities, but when law enforcement quickly acts on tips from private citizens (as happened in this instance) and follows through with their investigations, suspicious or illegal or terrorist activity can be countered.

THE FLOW OF INFORMATION

Gathering information and analyzing it for threat possibilities is a large part of the DHS's job. Once a threat is found to be real and credible, getting the threat information to those in the area of the threat is the top priority. The people getting this information include state and local officials, first responders, and the National Guard.

When the information is passed to the first responders, they put into action their protection and prevention plans. These plans have been in place for many years. They are actually part of the normal day-to-day routine of readiness preparation for police, fire, and emergency rescue departments across the nation. Unfortunately, many local and state first responders do not have training in biological, chemical, and nuclear threats. The Department of Homeland Security has promised to fund this training. Yet, these funds have not come down to those first responders.

FUNDING FOR FIRST RESPONDERS

First responders are the people who do much of the day-to-day work involved in securing the homeland and responding to attacks. The most obvious are police officers, firefighters, and emergency medical technicians from area hospitals. Other first responders include public health labs, which are responsible for responding to chemical or biological attacks. Every city and town public emergency agency is also considered a first-response unit in the war on terrorism and homeland defense.

The Bush administration promised a $3.5 billion budget in 2002 for first responders nationwide. Only $750 million in federal funds

INTELLIGENCE COMMUNICATION MISTAKE STRIKES AGAIN

A group of people rush away from the Capitol after being evacuated on June 9, 2004.

On June 9, 2004, a top general at the North American Aerospace Defense Command (NORAD) ordered fighter jets to intercept an unidentified plane that had crossed into Washington, D.C., airspace, headed for the Capitol. The general was reported by news agencies to have been ready to order the plane shot down. Fortunately, the general did not issue the order, as the plane turned out to carry Kentucky governor Ernie Fletcher. The communication mishap occurred because the governor's plane had a malfunctioning transponder, which issues identification radio signals. The pilot, as required, notified the FAA of the problem, but the FAA did not pass the information on to NORAD. Even if the shoot-down order had been given, the Associated Press reported, the jets were too far away to intercept the plane if it had indeed been ready to attack the Capitol. Representative Jim Turner, the top Democrat on the House Homeland Security Committee, had this to say: "The incident raises the question: Does the existing no-fly zone around our nation's capitol give sufficient time to intercept terrorist-controlled flight? Further, it appears that the FAA miscommunicated with other agencies responsible for the protection of Washington."

Nearly three years after the 9/11 attacks, miscommunication between government agencies continues to put Americans at risk

became available to the nation's first responders. The rest of the needed money, according to the Bush administration, must come from the states themselves. However, the nation was still in a deep recession in 2002. Tax dollars were scarce, people were out of work, and public treasuries across the country did not have the money for all the needs proposed by President Bush and the Department of Homeland Security.

Critics argued that big plans were made, but little of the funds trickled down to those who needed it most. Their criticism was backed by real figures gathered from federal, state, and local governments, as well as those public agencies that would be doing the work of first response to terrorist threats or attacks. For example, the think tank called Foreign Policy in Focus (FPIF) issued a report on September 9, 2003, criticizing the funding of the Bush administration's war in Iraq over the needs of homeland security. The report claimed, "Funds are needed to place essential

New York City police officer Patrick Ketcham patrols Grand Central Terminal on February 13, 2003, with his K-9 dog, Max. New York City is often cited in the federal government's terror alerts. The city has been on a high terror alert since 9/11.

equipment in the hands of emergency personnel and provide them with appropriate training." The FPIF also culled reports from the nation's police, fire, and other public-safety agencies to assess their needs and deficiencies. The following is a sample of their findings.

■ The National Fire Protection Association claims that, nationwide, fire departments can only equip half their firefighters with radios on any given shift; there are only enough breathing apparatuses for a third of each shift; and only 10 percent of fire departments have the people and equipment to respond to a building collapse.

■ During major emergencies, the communications systems are inadequate for America's 73,000 police, fire, and other public-safety agencies to be able to communicate with each other.

■ Most cities (both large and small) do not have the needed equipment to determine the type of hazardous materials first responders may be facing.

■ Most states' public health labs do not have needed equipment or skills to respond capably to a chemical or biological attack.

■ Only two state labs are able to test for biotoxins, while thirty-nine states reported that their labs could not safely accept samples of hazardous materials for testing.

■ Two years after 9/11, there has still been no fully equipped and monitored training exercise to test local and national readiness in the event of a chemical attack.

According to the critics, these examples of poor readiness due to a lack of funds show a lack of will by the federal government to find the money necessary for what it describes as a top priority for the nation. Moreover, the Bush administration's 2004 budget plans to cut $2 billion from crime prevention and public safety programs. Also, in the federal budget for 2003 to 2004, only $27 billion has been earmarked for emergency responders over the next five years. That amounts to a little more than $5 billion per year. Local and state governments plan to spend up to three times that figure for the same time frame. Yet, as the FPIF reports:

> Professional associations of emergency responders and leading emergency response officials from around the country estimate that these planned expenditures fall roughly $100 billion short of what's needed to [ensure] that emergency responders have the training and equipment they need to respond to future terrorist attacks. This shortfall of $20 billion per year represents a few months of funding for the $1 billion per week occupation in Iraq.

PUBLIC SAFETY, HOMELAND SECURITY, AND POLITICS

Critics rightfully ask the question, "Does every small town need the same equipment as the major metropolitan cities in America?" Probably not, as terrorists or even another country leveling an attack on the United States would likely hit a large city instead of a rural area. Yet preparedness means that minimum standards must be set to ensure some level of preparedness and competence among emergency responders.

On June 30, 2003, the Council on Foreign Relations released a report in which it concluded: "The United States has not reached a sufficient level of emergency preparedness and remains dangerously unprepared to handle a catastrophic attack on American soil, particularly one involving chemical, biological, radiological, or nuclear agents or coordinated high-impact conventional means."

Elaborating on the report during a PBS *NewsHour* interview that day, the chairperson of the council, former senator Warren Rudman, said:

> We took a number of months talking to every emergency group in America: police chiefs, firemen, fire chiefs associations, hospitals, emergency medical technicians, and so forth. And we simply asked the question: if a chemical or biological attack were to occur, or a nuclear or radiological attack, are you prepared to deal with it? The answer was universally "no."

Richard Clarke, National Security Council chief for terrorism during the Clinton administration and the first year of the Bush presidency, also participated in the *NewsHour* interview. In response to a question on what kind of spending priorities must occur to bring the most basic needs of the country up to acceptable levels, he said:

> The problem is that there's no process. There's no way that the Congress can answer the question, how much is enough? There's no way that Congress can answer the question, if I add 10 percent, what more do I get for it? And what we're recommending is that the Congress require of the administration a process, so that we can quantify our goals and quantify how far along we are rather than yelling at each other.
>
> The Department of Homeland Security said today we inflated the numbers, we were talking about gold-plated telephones. There's no point in arguing about the numbers. We need a process that allows us all to see how we get those numbers and allows the Congress to say, "I'm willing to assume this amount of risk but not that amount of risk." We don't have that kind of process today, so the Congress is forced to guess on how much money is enough.

The Bush administration is doing its own accounting, however, and many critics see pork-barrel spending. This means that money is spent on special projects put forward by particular people for their home state, city, or even local town. The most glaring example is the amount of money spent on homeland security as a percentage of the number of people living in the state. Wyoming receives $10 per person from the Department of Homeland Security for emergency preparedness. On the other hand, New York State, site of the 9/11 attacks, the nation's financial capital, and home to several nuclear power plants and important sea ports, gets only $1.40 per person to bring the state up to a much higher standard of preparedness. Critics note that Wyoming is the home state of Vice President Dick Cheney, which probably accounts for the disparity in funding between the two states. They say that this kind of favoritism in the highest reaches of the U.S. government makes the rest of the country, and its most vital services against terrorist threats, suffer from Washington politics.

Naturally, first responders will still respond to any threat or attack. This is what these people do out of duty, pride, and a real sense of patriotism. Without the needed funds to get them the required equipment to do their jobs, however, the possibility of another terrorist attack is high. And without that equipment, training, and preparedness, the effect may be hundreds if not thousands of casualties.

Richard A. Clarke

PREPARATIONS FOR ATTACK: WEAPONS OF MASS DESTRUCTION

Many critics, analysts, and government officials have said that the hijacked planes of 9/11 were themselves weapons of mass destruction. Flying a fully fueled jet airplane at 600 miles per hour (966 kilometers per hour) into a skyscraper or other building proved that they are correct. Nearly 3,000 people died during those attacks. Yet this use of airplanes as weapons is unconventional.

Former National Security Council chief Richard Clarke testified before the bipartisan 9/11 Commission on March 24, 2004. He was the only Bush administration official to accept any responsibility for the government's failure to prevent the 9/11 attacks.

Usually, weapons of mass destruction include chemical, biological, nuclear, and radiological weapons. These weapons have the potential of killing thousands. In the case of nuclear weapons, hundreds of thousands of people could die from a single suitcase-size bomb set off in a metropolitan area. This does not include the devastation to the environment, which would not be usable for hundreds or thousands of years because of high radiation left behind from the blast.

The real threat of chemical, biological, or nuclear attack is now with the United States every day. The country is vulnerable to the activities of terrorists trying to enter the country and to those who may already be here, waiting to strike.

Director of the National Security Agency Lt. Gen. Michael Hayden, CIA director George Tenet, and FBI director Robert Mueller raise their hands as they are sworn in before a joint House and Senate Select Intelligence Committee hearing on October 17, 2002. The limited cooperation between the nation's intelligence agencies has often been cited as a significant hurdle to overcome in improving homeland security.

HOW SAFE IS AMERICA?

Much of the criticism of the Department of Homeland Security seems to hinge on the amount of money available for all the various agencies, programs, and proposals now in place. One might ask why money has anything to do with safety, as it is people, government, and technology that must do the job of protecting the United States from further attack.

Unfortunately, in today's world, nothing can be done without paying for it. Those needed walkie-talkies for first responders cost money. Salaries paid to first responders cost money. Money is needed to design and build vehicles and weapons and to deploy and feed army personnel.

Of course, money itself could not have prevented the 9/11 hijackers from succeeding in their goals. The intelligence and transportation safety apparatuses had failed. But intelligence and safety measures cannot prevent terrorism all the time without the proper funding that so many critics are now pointing out is lacking in present and near-future budgets to prepare and keep Americans safe. Ultimately, the combination of people, intelligence, equipment, leadership, and the money to pay for the best of all these is the only option for the future of homeland security.

9/11 COMMISSION RECOMMENDATIONS

For sixteen months, a special Congressional commission looking into the September 11, 2001, attacks interviewed hundreds of people. These interviews included former president Bill Clinton and sitting president George W. Bush. On July 22, 2004, the commission published its final report. In it, the commission placed no blame on specific people or either of the presidents in office during the Al Qaeda attacks on American interests between 1992 and 2001. However, the commission criticized Congress, Clinton, and Bush for their

> "We believe we are safer today. But we are not safe."
>
> *9/11 Commission*

failure to protect the American people from attack.

The commission report documented intelligence failures over a decade-long period and noted the federal post-9/11 efforts to improve homeland security. It declared: "Because of offensive actions against

Al Qaeda since 9/11, and defensive actions to improve homeland security, we believe we are safer today. But we are not safe."

More important, the report included a number of sweeping recommendations for changes in the government in order to prevent further attacks. The commission called for the reorganization of domestic intelligence programs within the FBI so that information can move quickly to the top-level command within the agency. Further, an office in the White House should be opened that would oversee intelligence gathering among fifteen intelligence agencies. Finally, the commission called for a national intelligence director, who would sit as a cabinet member in the White House and control the flow of information to the president.

Immediately, officials at the Pentagon and in the CIA, Secretary of Homeland Security Tom Ridge, and others in Congress opposed such sweeping changes. It seems such changes will set up turf wars in terms of who controls what information and power when it comes to national intelligence. Critics argue that this kind of opposition to change is what caused the intelligence failures in the first place. Members of the 9/11 Commission, for their part, vowed to take their recommendations to the people of the United States to help bring about their recommended changes. ■

GLOSSARY

Al Qaeda Arabic for "the base"; a worldwide terrorist organization once based in Taliban-controlled Afghanistan.

antidote A drug that works against a virus or germ after either has already infected an individual.

biological weapons Weapons based on the use of germs or viruses found in nature or manufactured in the laboratory, including anthrax, bubonic plague, and smallpox.

budget The amount of money available for a specific agency or purpose; a plan for using that money.

catastrophic Disastrous.

central nervous system The part of the nervous system that consists of the brain and the spinal cord.

chemical weapons Weapons based on the use of chemical combinations manufactured in a laboratory, including sarin, mustard gas, and other nerve agents.

consolidate To join together into one whole.

diagnostics The methods used to identify a disease from its signs and symptoms.

directorate A group or agency formed to organize and carry out government plans.

first responders People who are the first on the scene of an accident or catastrophe, be it naturally caused or coming from attack. These people include police, firefighters, emergency medical technicians, and other emergency response organization members.

hierarchy A chain of command.

hijack To take control by use of force of an airplane, automobile, or ship.

immigration The act of moving into a foreign country to live.

incubation period The period between infection with a germ and the appearance of the disease it causes.

intelligence Information concerning a rival or enemy or potential enemy.

metropolitan Relating to a major city.

municipality A city, town, or village that has its own local government.

naturalization The process by which a foreign immigrant becomes a citizen of a country.

nuclear weapons Weapons based on the use of radioactive substances detonated with the use of explosives.

organism An individual form of life, such as an animal, plant, or bacterium.

radiation sickness Any of a number of health problems resulting from exposure to radioactive material.

respiratory system The integrated system of organs involved in taking in oxygen and giving off carbon dioxide. It consists of the nasal passages, larynx, trachea, bronchial tubes, and lungs.

terrorist A person who uses violence or the threat of violence to strike fear in people.

vaccine A drug that when ingested prevents harm from a virus or germ.

vulnerable At risk for harm.

weapons of mass destruction Weapons that have the potential to kill hundreds or thousands of people during a single attack.

white supremacist A person of the Caucasian race who dislikes people of other races.

FOR MORE INFORMATION

Center for Nonproliferation Studies
460 Pierce Street
Monterey, CA 93940
(831) 647-4154
e-mail: cns@miis.edu
Web site: http://cns.miis.edu

Federation of American Scientists
1717 K Street NW, Suite 209
Washington, DC 20036
Web site: http://www.fas.org/index.html

Foreign Policy in Focus
733 15 Street NW, Suite 1020
Washington, DC 20005
(202) 234-9382
Web site: http://www.fpif.org

National Council on U.S.-Arab Relations
1140 Connecticut Avenue NW, Suite 1210
Washington, DC 20036
(202) 293-0801
Web site: http://www.ncusar.org

The United Nations
First Avenue at 46th Street
New York, NY 10017
Web site: http://www.un.org/english

U.S. Department of Homeland Security
Washington, DC 20528
Web site: http://www.dhs.gov/dhspublic/index.jsp

Web Sites

Due to the changing nature of Internet links, the Rosen Publishing Group, Inc., has developed an online list of Web sites related to the subject of this book. This site is updated regularly. Please use this link to access the list:

http://www.rosenlinks.com/lwmd/hswmd

[FOR FURTHER] READING

McCuen, Gary E. *Biological Terrorism and Weapons of Mass Destruction*. New York: GEM/McCuen Publications, 1999.

Payan, Gregory. *Chemical and Biological Weapons: Anthrax and Sarin*. New York: Scholastic, 2000.

Ranum, Marcus J. *The Myth of Homeland Security*. New York: John Wiley & Sons, 2003.

Roleff, Tamara L. *America Under Attack*. New York: Lucent Books, 2002.

Torr, James D. *Homeland Security*. New York: Gale Group, 2004.

Urban Terrorism. Amy E. Sadler and Paul A. Winters, eds. New York: Gale Group, 1996.

Weapons of Mass Destruction, What You Should Know: A Citizen's Guide to Biological, Chemical, and Nuclear Agents and Weapons. Gladson I. Nwanna, ed. New York: Frontline Publishers, 2004.

[BIBLIOGRAPHY]

Corn, David. "Homeland Insecurity." *The Nation*. Retrieved February 5, 2004 (http://www.thenation.com/doc.mhtml?I=20030922&s=corn).

Gershman, John. "Bush's Homeland Insecurity." *Foreign Policy in Focus*. Retrieved January 28, 2004 (http://www.fpif.org/commentary/ 2003/0309emergency.html).

"Homeland Security." Numerous articles retrieved from PBS.org on February 5, 2004 (http://www.pbs.org/search/search_results.html?q=homeland+ security&btnG.x=0&btnG.y=0&neighborhood=none).

Jeahl, Douglas. "Ex-CIA Aides Ask for Leak Inquiry by Congress." Retrieved January 22, 2004 (http://www.nytimes.com/2004/01/22/ politics/22INTE.html).

Labaton, Stephen. "Easing of Internet Regulations Challenges Surveillance Efforts." Retrieved January 22, 2004 (http://www.nytimes.com/ 2004/01/22/technology/22VOIC.html).

Mann, Charles C. "Homeland Insecurity," *The Atlantic Monthly*, September 2002.

Rashbaum, William K., and Judith Miller. "New York Police Take Broad Steps in Facing Terror." Retrieved February 16, 2004 (http://www.nytimes.com/ 2004/02/15/nyregion/15THREAT.html).

INDEX

ABOUT THE AUTHOR

Mark Beyer is the author of more than a dozen books on people, history, government, social sciences, and sports, and he has edited anthologies of nonfiction literature on both world wars. He is also a fiction author and a literary critic, whose column "Cover to Cover" appears in the *Tampa Tribune*'s *Flair* magazine. You can read some of those reviews at his Web site, http://www.bibliogrind.com.

PHOTO CREDITS

Cover © USCG/Mike Hvozda-Handout/Reuters/Corbis; pp. 4–5, 25, 30, 33, 43 © Reuters/Corbis; pp. 7, 16–17, 20, 22, 29, 40, 42, 45, 46–47, 51 © AP/Wide World Photos; p. 9 © Mark Wilson/Getty Images; pp. 12, 37, 38, 52–53 © Hulton/Archive/Getty Images; p. 14 © Henny Ray Abrahms/Reuters/Corbis; p. 15 courtesy of the Department of Homeland Security; p. 23 © NewsCom; p. 26 www.ready.gov/make_a_kit.html; p. 31 © Kim Kulish/Corbis; p. 32–33 © Lynsey Addario/Corbis; © p. 35 Larry Mulvehill/Photo Researchers.

Designer: Evelyn Horovicz; Editor: Wayne Anderson:
Photo Researcher: Sheri Liberman